Raggedy Ann & Andy's

RAGGEDY DOG'S BONE

P9-BYG-558

A LYNX BOOK

This book is published by Lynx Books, a division of Lynx Communications, Inc., 41 Madison Avenue, New York, New York 10010. The name "Lynx" together with the logotype consisting of a stylized head of a lynx is a trademark of Lynx Communications, Inc.

Raggedy Ann and Andy's Grow-and-Learn Library, the names and depictions of Raggedy Ann, Raggedy Andy and all related characters are trademarks of Macmillan, Inc.

MARCELLA'S HOUSE

PLAYHOUSE

TOOL SHED

PLAYROOM

This book belongs to:

_____

Raggedy Dog wanted a real bone, the kind of bone that real dogs have. It's true that Raggedy Dog was a toy dog, but he wanted a real bone anyway. He did not want a wooden bone. He did not want a rubber bone. He wanted a real bone, and he didn't know where to find one.

"Maybe there's a real bone in the toy box," Raggedy Dog said to himself. So he looked into the box. But all he saw was a pink ribbon. He picked it up in his mouth and wondered why there was a pink ribbon in the toy box.

JIGSAW PUZZLE 500 PIECES

"Oh, thank you," exclaimed Babette the French Doll.
"I've been looking all over for my favorite pink ribbon."
And Babette gave Raggedy Dog a little kiss on the nose.
"You're wonderful," she said.

"If I were wonderful," Raggedy Dog thought to
himself, "I'd have a real bone, the kind of bone that real
dogs have."

Raggedy Dog sat and thought for a while. Then he turned himself around and thought some more. Finally, he decided that the only thing to do was to look outside. Surely *outside* was where a dog who was looking for a real bone would look!

Raggedy Dog ran out the door and behind the house, heading toward the vegetable garden. He went right past the toolshed. He stopped and thought. Maybe the toolshed was a good out-of-the-way place to look for a bone. He pushed open the door and peeked inside.

Raggedy Dog saw a rake, a hoe, three flowerpots and a lawn mower. And he saw something odd behind the lawn mower. It was white and long. It was . . .

Raggedy Andy's hat!

"Raggedy Andy was playing hide-and-seek in the toolshed and must have lost his hat," Raggedy Dog said to himself.

Raggedy Dog was miserable. He marched out of the toolshed, right to where Raggedy Andy was playing. He dropped the hat at Raggedy Andy's feet.

"Wow!" said Raggedy Andy. "I didn't even notice that I had lost my hat. Thanks, Raggedy Dog. You sure can find anything!"

This made Raggedy Dog even more unhappy than before. If he could find *anything*, as Raggedy Andy said he could, why couldn't he find a real bone for himself, the kind of bone that the real dogs have?

Raggedy Dog kept looking and looking. Finally, he
saw something white under the porch. He ran across the
yard. Raggedy Dog sank his teeth into the tip and pulled.

It wasn't a bone. It was Marcella's baton!

Raggedy Dog knew that Marcella would never find her baton hidden under the porch. He pulled it out a little farther and left it where she would be sure to see it.

Raggedy Dog could find what everyone else was missing. Why couldn't he find the one thing that was so important to him?

Raggedy Dog stretched out under the apple tree. He guessed that maybe the reason he couldn't find a real bone was that he wasn't a real dog. He felt very sad. He wondered how real dogs knew where to look for real bones.

Then Raggedy Dog noticed something funny about the dirt near him. It was piled in a little mound. He wondered what was making the dirt stick up so much. So Raggedy Dog went over to find out.

Raggedy Dog pushed the dirt aside. He could not believe his eyes. There, right in the dirt, was a real bone! Raggedy Dog had never imagined that bones grew in the dirt! Now he guessed that maybe the bones grew up in little mounds just before they popped out of the ground. He took his brand-new bone and went back under the tree.

Raggedy Dog was very happy now.

Just then Fido came into the yard. Fido was Marcella's real dog. Raggedy Dog was Fido's favorite doll in Marcella's playroom. But this day, Fido did not come over to see Raggedy Dog. Instead, he went right to the patch of dirt near where Raggedy Dog was sitting. Fido started to dig in the dirt.

"I know what he's looking for," Raggedy Dog said to himself. He knew Fido was trying to find a bone in the dirt, too.

Something inside Raggedy Dog told him to hide his own bone so Fido wouldn't find it. Raggedy Dog felt a little funny inside as he pushed his real bone behind the apple tree.

Fido dug and dug. He made big holes and little holes, deep holes and shallow holes. Raggedy Dog had never seen so many holes in his entire life. But there were no bones in any of them.

Raggedy Dog felt very lucky that he had found his
bone on the very first try.

Finally, Fido came over and stretched out on the grass
next to Raggedy Dog.

Fido looked very sad.

"I just don't understand it," Fido barked at Raggedy Dog. "Yesterday I buried a bone right here in the dirt, and now it's gone."

Raggedy Dog sneaked a look over at the bone he had hidden behind the apple tree. Could this be the bone Fido had buried? Raggedy Dog thought about how much he had wanted a real bone, the kind of bone that real dogs have. He thought about how hard he had looked for the one he had finally found.

He also knew now that bones didn't grow in the ground. His bone was only there because Fido had buried it there. If Raggedy Dog gave the bone back, he wouldn't know where to look for another one.

Raggedy Dog didn't know what to do. He felt as if he should give the bone back, but he really wanted to keep it. Raggedy Dog looked at Fido's sad face. Then he looked again at the bone.

Very slowly he got up and walked behind the apple tree. He picked up the bone and dropped it in front of Fido.

Fido wasn't unhappy anymore. He jumped up and wagged his tail. He picked up the bone and barked a quick thanks to Raggedy Dog.

Raggedy Dog was glad that Fido was happy, but he didn't feel very happy himself.

After Fido left, Raggedy Dog sat back down under the apple tree. He knew he would have been unhappy if he had not told the truth. But he was still pretty unhappy now.

Raggedy Dog tried to think of something else that would make him happy besides a real bone, but he couldn't think of one single thing. He tried to think of someplace else to look for a real bone. But he was sure that, even if he found one, it would turn out to belong to some other real dog.

Raggedy Dog headed back toward the house. His ears were drooping. His tail was drooping. His eyes and mouth looked droopy, too.

Fido looked up from the bone and saw Raggedy Dog crossing the yard. Fido thought about how slowly Raggedy Dog had walked when he went behind the tree to get the bone. Then he understood how Raggedy Dog was feeling.

Fido crossed the yard to meet him. "Let's share the bone," Fido barked.

Raggedy Dog's ears and tail perked up.

"If you hadn't found the bone," Fido continued, "I wouldn't have it either. This will be *our* bone," he said kindly.

Raggedy Dog and Fido went back under the apple tree.
Fido dropped the bone right between them on the grass.
Raggedy Dog could not remember when he felt happier.
Not only did he have a real bone like a real dog has, but he
had a real dog to share it with, too!

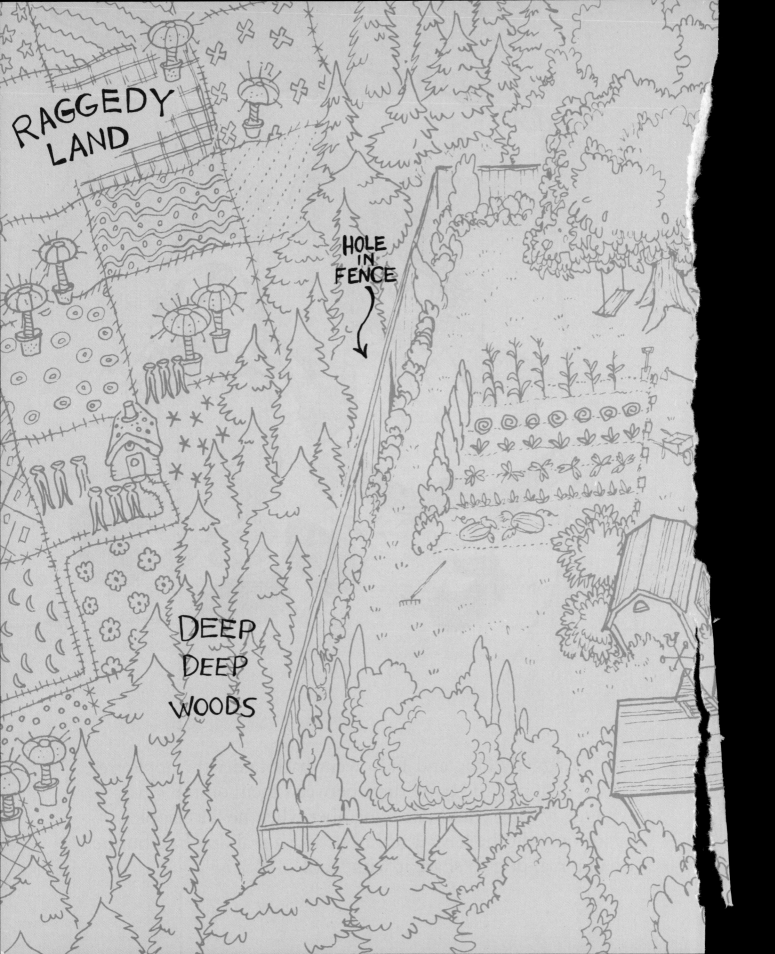